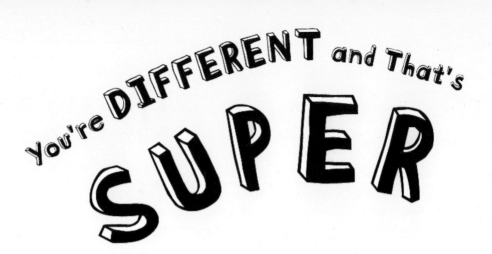

You're DIFFERENT and That's SUPER

Carson Kressley

Illustrated by Jared Lee

SIMON AND SCHUSTER

London • New York • Toronto • Sydney

SIMON AND SCHUSTER
First published in 2005 by Simon & Schuster Books for Young Readers
an imprint of Simon & Schuster Children's Publishing Division, New York

First published in Great Britain in 2006 by Simon & Schuster UK Ltd
Africa House, 64-78 Kingsway, London WC2B 6AH

Book design by Einav Aviram
The text for this book is set in Gill Sans

A CIP catalogue record for this book is available
from the British Library upon request

ISBN 1 416 91737 3
EAN 9781416917373

Printed in China
10 9 8 7 6 5 4 3 2 1

To my grandmother, Pauline Kressley, who wanted every kid to have a pony.

And thanks to my family, who thinks I'm super, even though I am different. To my friends, who told me the same. And to Richard Abate, Jennifer Joel, and the Simon & Schuster peeps, who made this all happen. – C. K.

To my daughter, Jana, who loves horses – J. L.

THE SPRING THAT TRUMPET WAS BORN, there were so many new foals in the pasture that almost no one noticed there was one sassy little colt who didn't belong to any of the mares.

For the most part, the foals born that spring were like those born every year before — some were dappled and some had stars between their eyes; some were frisky and some were shy.

But the little orphan colt was different. He had a coat that was as white as falling snow, a mane as golden as summer sunshine, and a whinny so loud and so clear that everyone took to calling him Trumpet.

Not a soul knew where Trumpet had come from. But he could run as swiftly and jump as high as any of the foals. So the mares just shrugged their shoulders and took the little scamp in.

And for that first year, Trumpet was just like all the other "kids".
They frolicked and raced through the summer.

In the autumn they discovered scrum-diddly-umptious
apples together.

And when the winter snow fell, they slept nuzzled together in the big red barn. Looked after by all the mares and treated like a brother by all his friends, Trumpet was easily the most popular colt around.

The trouble started on the morning of Trumpet's first birthday, when a bump began to grow at the top of his forehead.

At first the bump hid under Trumpet's bushy forelock, so nobody noticed what was happening.

But before long it poked through his hairdo.

"Icky," he heard Sunshine whisper when she thought he couldn't hear.

"And weird!" Tuckabuckaway whinnied back.

But the bump grew and grew,

and by the time autumn arrived, it had become a full-fledged horn!

A horn that got caught in the low branches of the apple tree during races in the meadow . . .

. . . and accidentally poked Wooligan in the eye.

After that, Sunshine told Trumpet that he couldn't play with them anymore.

All of Trumpet's besties looked at him like he was some
sort of hideous beast. So Trumpet began to spend his time
alone. He avoided the cool shade of the apple tree in the
pasture and moved down to the last stall in the barn.

Every night his head was the first to hit
the hay (and the only one with a horn!).

Still the others whispered about him.

"What's wrong with him?" they asked one another when they thought Trumpet couldn't hear them.

What is wrong with me? Trumpet asked himself.

I don't want to be different.

Different is awful.

Then one night Trumpet awoke to the sound of nervous

whinnying. The barn was full of smoke!

At the far end two mares were trying to stamp out a fire, but the flames were spreading quickly under their hooves. All the other ponies were rearing, clamouring and pawing at the barn doors. But they wouldn't budge. Through the crack between the doors, the ponies could see that the latch was securely fastened. Even the smallest, pony-size hooves and snouts were too big to fit through the narrow space and open it.

And at that precise moment Trumpet knew it was good to be different. He pushed through the other ponies, . . .

. . . poked his horn between the doors, and began to raise the latch.

It was harder than it looked. The barn was burning, and the other ponies were crowded around and pushing.

When the latch finally came free, the barn doors swung open,

and Trumpet and all his friends sprang out into the chilly night.

By the time the farmer reached the barn, everyone was safe.

But how did they get the doors open? he wondered.

Then, for the first time, the farmer noticed Trumpet.

The rest, if you will, is history. After the local news ran the story, everybody wanted to see the real, live unicorn — because the farmer could clearly see that Trumpet *was* a unicorn.

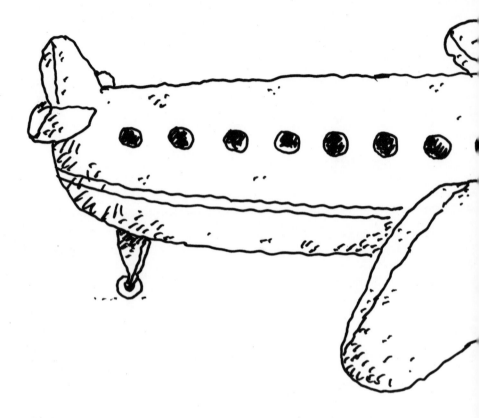

Suddenly, being different was super. And soon Trumpet was travelling all over the world. Making new friends and causing a sensation. Being a famous, one-of-a-kind, too-good-to-be-true, can-you-believe-it wonder.

After Trumpet was whisked away, things at the stable just weren't the same.

But maybe they'll be different again . . .

... come the spring.

...come the spring